Blessings!
Love
Valerie

For Charlotte V.T.
For Connor, Chloe, Joe, Anya and Ethan M.M.

Text by Victoria Tebbs
Illustrations copyright © 2006 Melanie Mitchell
This edition copyright © 2006 Lion Hudson

The moral rights of the author and illustrator
have been asserted

A Lion Children's Book
an imprint of
Lion Hudson plc
Mayfield House, 256 Banbury Road,
Oxford OX2 7DH, England
www.lionhudson.com
ISBN-13: 978 0 7459 4901 7
ISBN-10: 0 7459 4901 0

First edition 2006
1 3 5 7 9 10 8 6 4 2 0

A catalogue record for this book is available
from the British Library

Typeset in 36/40 Baskerville MT Schoolbook
Printed and bound in Singapore

See and Say!
Noah's Ark Story

Victoria Tebbs

Illustrated by Melanie Mitchell

LION
CHILDREN'S

Here are the bad people.

biff boff baff

Here is Noah. He is good and kind.

hmmm hmmm

God tells Noah to build a big boat.

bang, bang

All the animals go on Noah's boat.

Soon it starts to rain.

pitter patter

The boat begins to float.

splish splosh

There's more rain. Lots of rain.

Then the rain stops. The water goes down.

gurgle gurgle

Noah is happy. His family are happy. The animals are happy too. The water has all gone now.

Hurrah!

Look – a pretty rainbow in the sky. God's world is new again.

Hooray!

purr